Let's Find Ads on TV

by Mari Schuh

first step nonfiction

Lerner Publications ◆ Minneapolis

The images in this book are from: © Jim Watson/AFP/Getty Images, p. 4; © iStockphoto.com/Richard Legg, p. 5; © iStockphoto.com/Peeter Viisimaa, p. 6; © iStockphoto.com/Anatolii Babii, p. 7 (background); marioparty10.nintendo.com, p. 7 (inset); © iStockphoto.com/PeopleImages, p. 8; © Onoky/SuperStock, p. 9; © iStockphoto.com/DragonImages, p. 10; © shock/Bigstock.com, p. 11 (background); Little Caesar's Pizza ad, p. 11 (inset); © TatyanaGl/Bigstock.com, p. 12 (background); Fruit Loops Bloopers ad, p. 12 (inset); © iStockphoto.com/OJO_Images, p. 13; McDonald's ad, p. 14; © iStockphoto.com/s-cphoto, p. 15 (background); AP Photo/Ted S. Warren, p. 15 (inset); © Jakob Helbig/Cultura/Getty Images, p. 16; © Patrick Pleul/dpa/CORBIS, p. 17 (background); American Idol Prod./19 Television/FOX TV Network/Fremantle Media North America/Michael Becker/Kobal Collection/Art Resource, NY, p. 17 (inset); © Photographerlondon/Dreamstime.com, p. 18 (background); © Consumer Trends/Alamy, p. 18 (inset); © Chris Ryan/OJO Images Ltd/Alamy, p. 19; © Vicki Beaver/Alamy, p. 20; Juggle Bubbles ad, p. 21; © Thomas Northcut/Iconica/Getty Images, p. 22 (background); M&Ms ad, p. 22 (inset).
Cover: © Ariel Skelley/Blend Images/Getty Images.

Main body text set in ITC Avant Garde Gothic Std Medium 21/25.
Typeface provided by International Typeface Corp.

Lerner Publications Company
A division of Lerner Publishing Group, Inc.
241 First Avenue North
Minneapolis, MN 55401 USA

For reading levels and more information, look up this title at www.lernerbooks.com.

Library of Congress Cataloging-in-Publication Data

Schuh, Mari C., 1975–
Let's find ads on TV / by Mari Schuh.
pages cm. — (First step nonfiction : learn about advertising)
Includes index.
ISBN 978-1-4677-9466-4 (lb : alk. paper) — ISBN 978-1-4677-9663-7 (pb : alk. paper) — ISBN 978-1-4677-9664-4 (eb pdf)
1. Television advertising—Juvenile literature. I. Title.
HF6146.T42S338 2016
659.14'3—dc23 2015017901

Manufactured in the United States of America
1 – CG – 12/31/15

Table of Contents

What Is an Ad?

An **ad** tells people about a **product**.

An ad can make people want to buy the product.

An ad can be words on a sign. An ad can be a picture in a magazine.

This video tells about a game.

An ad can be a video on the Internet.

Companies use ads to sell their products.

TV Commercials

Some companies show ads on TV.

Many TV ads play during breaks in a show.

This commercial is selling pizza.

These ads are called **commercials**.

Commercials use videos and sounds to sell products.

Commercials show people using a product. They make products look fun.

An ad can make you want food.

Some commercials sell toys. Others sell food.

Products on TV Shows

Ads can also be part of a TV show.

Companies pay to have their products on TV shows.

These people are drinking from Coca-Cola cups. The cups are an ad.

TV characters use the product on the show.

Sometimes the characters talk about the product.

People might want to buy a product after they see an ad.

People watch the TV show. They see and hear about the product.

Thinking about Ads

Sometimes ads can make products seem better than they are.

Do you think this ad is true?

This ad says these bubbles won't pop.

What does this ad want you to think?

Glossary

ad – a message that tries to sell a product or a service

commercials – short ads that are shown during breaks in a TV show

companies – groups that make or sell products or services

product – an item that is made and sold

Index